RICKY RICOTTA'S

MIGHTY ROBOT

vs. THE MECHA-MONKEYS FROM MARS

STORY BY
DAV PILKEY

ART BY
DAN SANTAT

SCHOLASTIC INC.

FOR LEWIS AND LUCY BROCK
– D.P.

FOR LEAH
– D.S.

Text copyright © 2002, 2014 by Dav Pilkey
www.pilkey.com

Illustrations copyright © 2014 by Dan Santat
www.dantat.com

Library of Congress Cataloging-in-Publication Data

Pilkey, Dav, 1966 – author.
Ricky Ricotta's mighty robot vs. the mecha-monkeys from Mars /
story by Dav Pilkey ; art by Dan Santat. — Revised edition.
pages cm
Summary: A small mouse and his best friend, a giant flying robot, attempt to save
the Earth when an evil Martian monkey and his mechanical creations attack.
1. Ricotta, Ricky (Fictitious character) — Juvenile fiction. 2. Mice — Juvenile fiction.
3. Robots — Juvenile fiction. 4. Heroes — Juvenile fiction. 5. Monkeys — Juvenile fiction.
6. Mars (Planet) — Juvenile fiction. [1. Mice — Fiction. 2. Robots — Fiction. 3. Heroes —
Fiction. 4. Humorous stories.] I. Santat, Dan, illustrator. II. Title. III. Title: Ricky
Ricotta's mighty robot versus the mecha-monkeys from Mars.
PZ7.P63123Row 2014   813.54 — dc23   2014003713

ISBN 978-0-545-63012-2

12 11 10 9 8 7 6 5 4 3 2   14 15 16 17 18 19/0

Printed in China   38

Revised edition
First printing, July 2014

Book design by Phil Falco

CHAPTERS

CHAPTER ONE
THE BIG MISTAKE

One day, Ricky Ricotta and his Mighty Robot were playing hide-and-seek in their yard.

"This game is too easy," said Ricky. "Let's ride skateboards instead!"

Ricky got his skateboard out of the garage, but there was no skateboard big enough for his Mighty Robot.

"I know," said Ricky. "We can use
my parents' minivan!"

Soon, Ricky and his Mighty Robot were zooming down the street. "This is fun!" said Ricky.

But it stopped being
fun when they wiped out.

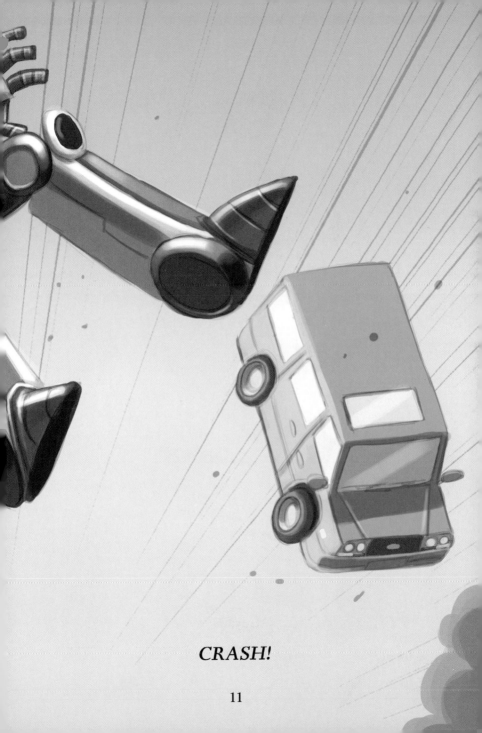

CRASH!

SPLASH!!!

When Ricky and his Robot
got out of the pond, they saw
the smashed-up minivan.

"Uh-oh," said Ricky. "We're in big trouble now!"

Ricky's Mighty Robot put the minivan back in the driveway.

"Maybe Mom and Dad won't notice," said Ricky.

But they did.

CHAPTER TWO
BIG TROUBLE

Ricky's mother and father were not happy.

"All right," said Ricky's father. "Which one of you boys squished our minivan?"

Ricky and his Mighty Robot looked down at the ground. They were very worried.

Finally, Ricky confessed.

"We both did," said Ricky. "It was an accident."

"You boys were very irresponsible," said Ricky's father.

"Yes," said Ricky's mother, "and you will have to find a way to pay for the damage you have done."

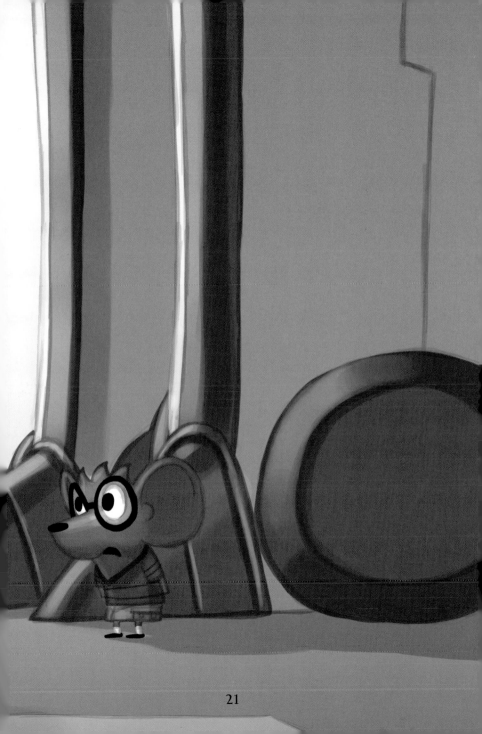

CHAPTER THREE
MAJOR MONKEY HATES MARS

Meanwhile, about 35 million miles away, on the planet Mars, there lived a mean little monkey who was hatching an evil plan.

His name was Major Monkey, and he hated living on Mars. Mars was a cold, dry, and very, very lonely place.

Major Monkey kept himself busy by building evil robots and strange machines in his secret laboratory, but he was still lonely.

There was nobody to talk to.
There was nobody to yell at. And,
worst of all, there was nobody to
be mean to.

So Major Monkey decided to take over the planet Earth and enslave all of mousekind.

Major Monkey had watched Earth for many months. He saw other evil villains try to take over the planet, but they were always stopped by Ricky Ricotta's Mighty Robot.

"I must get rid of that Mighty Robot!" said Major Monkey. "And I know just how to do it."

CHAPTER FOUR
THE TRAP

The next morning, as Ricky and his Mighty Robot walked to school, they tried to think of a way to pay for their mistake of wrecking the minivan.

"How many years will it take to buy a new minivan with my allowance?" asked Ricky.

Ricky's Robot used his super brain to figure out the answer.

"Hmmm," said Ricky. "Only 259 years? Maybe we should think of a better plan."

Suddenly, a small spaceship zoomed out of the sky. The top of the spaceship opened up, and a spacemouse peeked out.

"Help us! Help us!" cried the spacemouse. "Mars is under attack! We need your Mighty Robot to save us!"

Ricky Ricotta's Mighty Robot could not turn away from someone who needed help. So the Mighty Robot followed the tiny spaceship all the way to Mars.

"Be careful up there!" Ricky shouted.

CHAPTER FIVE
BETRAYED

Ricky's Mighty Robot soon arrived
on Mars. He saw a strange laboratory,
but he did not see any evil villains.

The Mighty Robot flew closer to the laboratory. Suddenly, a giant metal hand reached out of the hillside.

It grabbed Ricky's Robot and would not let go.

Ricky's Mighty Robot tried and tried, but he could not escape the grip of the giant metal hand.

Major Monkey looked up from
the spaceship and pulled a mask off
his head.

"*I tricked you! I tricked you!*"
Major Monkey mocked. "Now it is
YOU who needs help! Haw-haw-haw!"

Major Monkey pressed a button inside his spaceship. Soon, three giant Mecha-Monkeys rose from the depths of the strange laboratory.

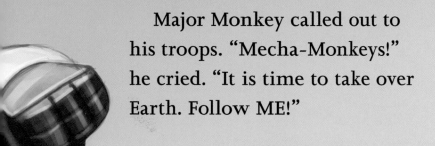

Major Monkey called out to his troops. "Mecha-Monkeys!" he cried. "It is time to take over Earth. Follow ME!"

CHAPTER SIX
MAJOR MONKEY MAKES HIS MOVE

Ricky was taking a spelling test when he saw the little spaceship return with three enormous Mecha-Monkeys.

"Hey," cried Ricky, "where's my Robot?"

"He got into a tight squeeze," laughed Major Monkey. "And he's never coming BACK — haw-haw-haw!"

CHAPTER SEVEN
THE MOUSE FROM SASA

Things were not looking good for Earth.

"If only my Mighty Robot were here," said Ricky. "He'd stop those crazy monkeys and save us all."

"Don't worry," said Ricky's father. "I'm sure he'll find a way to escape."

Soon, there was a knock on the front door. It was a general from the Squeakyville Air and Space Association.

"We are going to send a space shuttle up to Mars to rescue your Mighty Robot," said the general. "He is our only hope."

"Hooray!" cried Ricky.

"And we need you to come
with us, Ricky," said the general.
"You know that Robot better
than anybody."

"Can I go?" Ricky asked his parents. *"Pleeeeease?"*

"Well," said Ricky's father, "all right. But you must promise to be careful!"

"Hooray!" cried Ricky.

CHAPTER EIGHT
THE SPACE SHUTTLE

Ricky and his parents got into the general's car. The general turned on the rocket boosters, and they all flew straight to the Space Center.

"This is *so cool!*" said Ricky's father.

Soon, Ricky was sitting inside a giant space shuttle with three real astromice.

Ricky fastened his seat belt, and
off they blasted into outer space.

When the shuttle arrived on Mars, Ricky and the astromice saw Major Monkey's laboratory.

They saw the Mighty Robot trapped inside the giant metal hand. But what could they do?

Suddenly, another giant metal
hand reached out of the hillside and
grabbed the space shuttle.
  Then the strange laboratory began
to rise from the ground.

It rose higher and higher . . .

. . . until finally it stepped out of the ground. Major Monkey's laboratory had turned into a colossal Orangu-Tron.

The astromice inside the space shuttle tried to open the emergency exit door, but it was stuck.

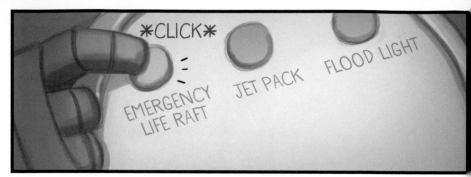

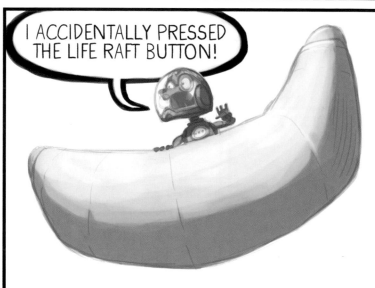

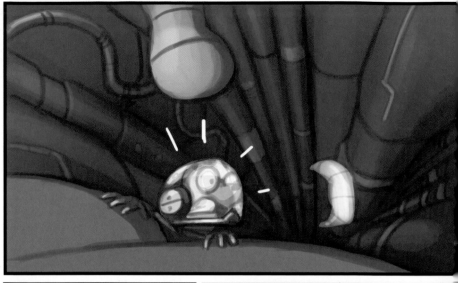

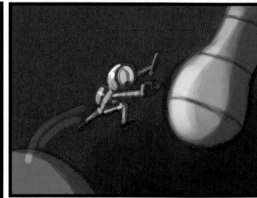

Ricky had found his way into a strange
control center. He looked around
nervously. He saw lots of evil robots
and many strange machines.

Then Ricky found the main power switch.
Ricky grabbed the switch and tried to
turn off the power, but the switch was stuck.
Ricky pulled and pulled on the switch.

Finally, Ricky was spotted by an evil Robo-Chimp.

"Destroy the intruder!" said the Robo-Chimp. "Destroy the intruder!"

The Robo-Chimp grabbed Ricky's breathing tube and started pulling. Soon, other Robo-Chimps joined in. Harder and harder they pulled.

Then Ricky got an idea. He wrapped his breathing tube around the main power switch and held on tight. The Robo-Chimps pulled and pulled. Finally, the switch began to move.

The harder the Robo-Chimps pulled, the more the switch moved.

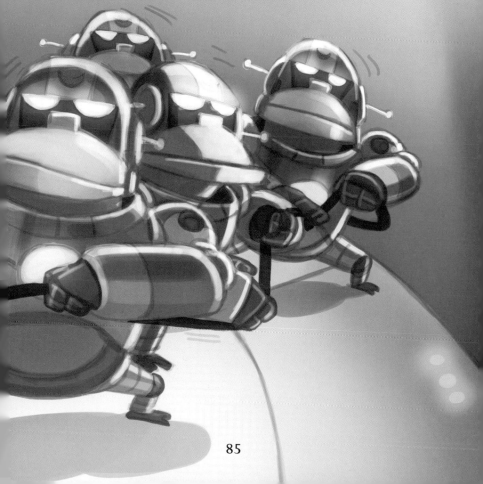

Ka-KLANK!

Suddenly, the power for the whole laboratory turned off.

"Hooray!" cried Ricky.

CHAPTER TEN
FREEDOM

Outside, the Orangu-Tron lost all of
its power. Ricky's Mighty Robot pushed
his way out of the giant metal hand.
He was free at last!

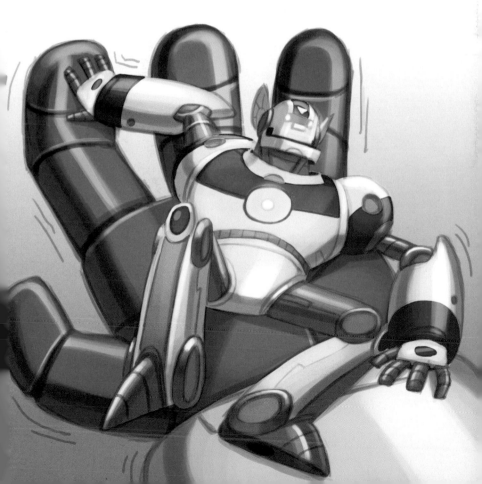

But inside, Ricky was in trouble. The Robo-Chimps rushed toward Ricky. "Must destroy intruder!" they chanted. "Must restore power!"

"HELP ME!" screamed Ricky as the Robo-Chimps came closer and closer.

KER-POW!

Ricky's Mighty Robot punched
a hole in the roof and grabbed
Ricky just in time.

Ricky pushed the SELF-DESTRUCT button. "Let's get out of here!" cried Ricky as the laboratory began to shake and crumble.

SELF-
DESTRUC
1:59

With Ricky in one hand and the space
shuttle in the other, Ricky's Mighty Robot
zoomed into space — just in time.

KA-BOOOOOOOOM!

"That takes care of Mars," said
Ricky. "Now we have to save Earth!"

CHAPTER ELEVEN
BACK TO EARTH

When they got back to Earth, Ricky's Mighty Robot spotted Major Monkey.

"Wh-What are *YOU* doing here?" asked Major Monkey.

"We're here to save Earth!" said Ricky.

"Oh, yeah?" said Major Monkey. "We'll see about that!" He called his Mecha-Monkeys and ordered them to destroy Ricky's Mighty Robot.

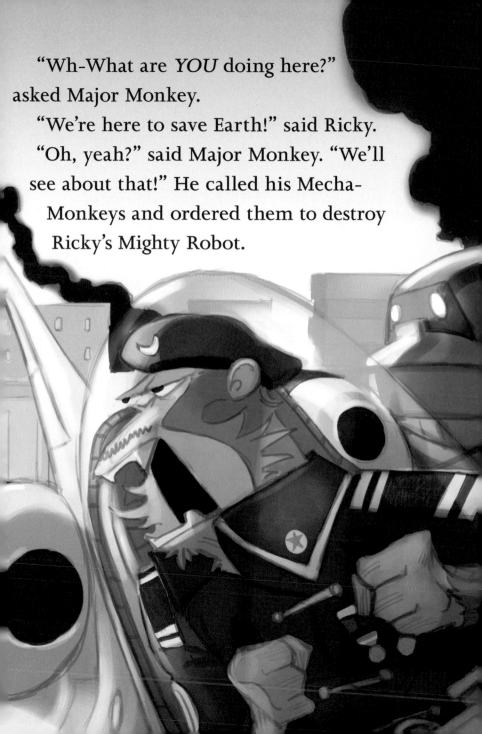

Ricky's Robot put Ricky and the space shuttle someplace safe. Then the robo-battle began.

Ricky's Robot treated the Mecha-Monkeys to two servings of *punch* . . .

. . . one *foot-long* . . .

. . . and a *knuckle sandwich.*

Major Monkey was very upset.
"All right, banana brains," he shouted.
"Quit monkeying around! Let's see
some action!"

CHAPTER TWELVE
THE BIG BATTLE
(IN FLIP-O-RAMA™)

-RAMA
HERE'S HOW IT WORKS!

STEP 1
Place your *left* hand inside the dotted lines marked "LEFT HAND HERE." Hold the book open *flat*.

STEP 2
Grasp the *right-hand* page with your right thumb and index finger (inside the dotted lines marked "RIGHT THUMB HERE").

STEP 3
Now *quickly* flip the right-hand page back and forth until the picture appears to be *animated*.

(For extra fun, try adding your own sound-effects!)

FLIP-O-RAMA 1

(pages 109 and 111)

Remember, flip *only* page 109.
While you are flipping, be sure you
can see the picture on page 109
and the one on page 111.
If you flip quickly, the two
pictures will start to look like
<u>one</u> *animated* picture.

Don't forget to add
your own sound-effects!

LEFT HAND HERE

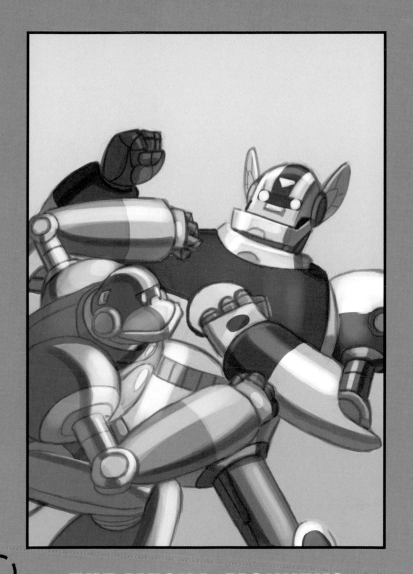

THE MECHA-MONKEYS ATTACKED.

RIGHT
THUMB
HERE

RIGHT
INDEX
FINGER
HERE

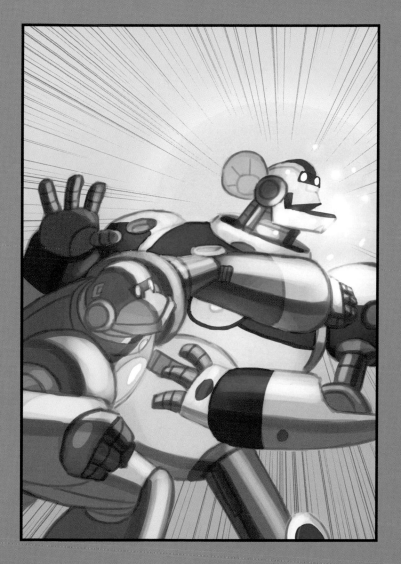

THE MECHA-MONKEYS ATTACKED.

FLIP-O-RAMA 2

(pages 113 and 115)

Remember, flip *only* page 113.
While you are flipping, be sure you
can see the picture on page 113
and the one on page 115.
If you flip quickly, the two
pictures will start to look like
<u>one</u> *animated* picture.

Don't forget to add
your own sound-effects!

LEFT HAND HERE

RICKY'S ROBOT
FOUGHT BACK.

RIGHT
THUMB
HERE

RIGHT
INDEX
FINGER
HERE

RICKY'S ROBOT
FOUGHT BACK.

FLIP-O-RAMA 3

(pages 117 and 119)

Remember, flip *only* page 117.
While you are flipping, be sure you
can see the picture on page 117
and the one on page 119.
If you flip quickly, the two
pictures will start to look like
<u>one</u> *animated* picture.

Don't forget to add
your own sound-effects!

LEFT HAND HERE

THE MECHA-MONKEYS
BATTLED HARD.

RIGHT
THUMB
HERE

THE MECHA-MONKEYS
BATTLED HARD.

FLIP-O-RAMA 4

(pages 121 and 123)

Remember, flip *only* page 121.
While you are flipping, be sure you
can see the picture on page 121
and the one on page 123.
If you flip quickly, the two
pictures will start to look like
<u>one</u> *animated* picture.

Don't forget to add
your own sound-effects!

LEFT HAND HERE

RICKY'S ROBOT
BATTLED HARDER.

RIGHT
THUMB
HERE

RIGHT
INDEX
FINGER
HERE

122

RICKY'S ROBOT
BATTLED HARDER.

FLIP-O-RAMA 5

(pages 125 and 127)

Remember, flip *only* page 125.
While you are flipping, be sure you
can see the picture on page 125
and the one on page 127.
If you flip quickly, the two
pictures will start to look like
<u>one</u> *animated* picture.

Don't forget to add
your own sound-effects!

LEFT HAND HERE

RICKY'S ROBOT
WON THE WAR.

RIGHT
THUMB
HERE

RIGHT
INDEX
FINGER
HERE

126

RICKY'S ROBOT
WON THE WAR.

CHAPTER THIRTEEN
PAYING FOR MISTAKES

Poor Major Monkey. His Mecha-Monkeys flew home to Mars, and he could not rule the world anymore.

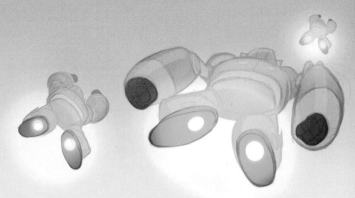

"Boo-hoo-hoo!" cried Major
Monkey. "I've made a big mistake."
"Yes," said Ricky. "And now you
must pay for your mistake!"

Together, the two heroes put Major Monkey where he belonged: in the Squeakyville jail.

"Thank you, boys, for saving Earth,"
said the general. "If there's anything
we can do to repay you, please let
me know!"

Ricky whispered in his Robot's ear.
The Robot nodded his giant head.

"Well, sir," said Ricky, "we sure
could use a new minivan."

"All right," said the general. "How many would you like?"

CHAPTER FOURTEEN

HEROES

Ricky and his Mighty Robot flew back to the Space Center to meet Ricky's parents.

"Mom! Dad!" cried Ricky. "Look what the general gave us. A brand-new minivan!"

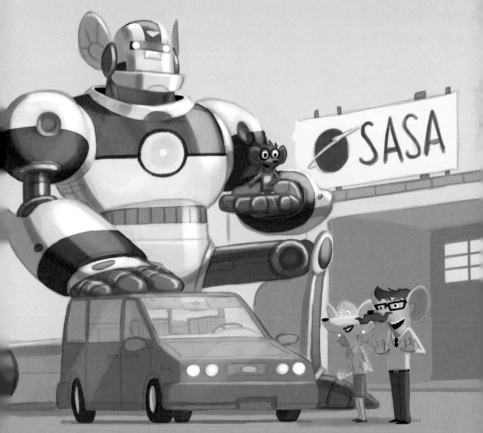

"Wow!" said Ricky's mother.

"We'll race you home!" said Ricky's father.

So Ricky Ricotta and his Mighty Robot raced the rocket-powered minivan all the way home.

Soon, the whole Ricotta family was safe at home eating cheese pizza and drinking root beer.

"Thank you for rescuing each other today," said Ricky's mother.

"Yes," said Ricky's father, "and thank you for paying for your mistake."

"No problem," said Ricky . . .

... "that's what friends are for!"

READY FOR

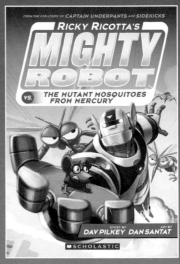

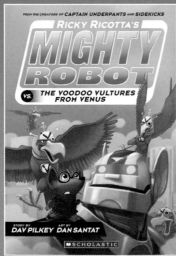

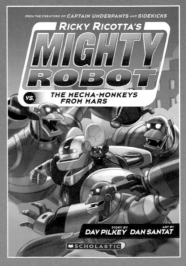